WHEN THE WOLVES HOWL

SIDRA KHAN

To My parents, my best friend and people working hard to save wildlife

Contents

CHAPTER ONE

The Hunt

Her white paws skidded through the fresh snow. Her blue eyes were fixed on her prey that was a reindeer. The young reindeer ran for its life, its hoofs skidded baches of snow on her nozzle, but she didn't stop.

She was near her prey; very nearby.

Just one more leap, just one more leap.

She leaped with her mouth open, ready to make her bite. But she fell, and the reindeer hit her with one kick and ran away.

She was a wolf, and her name was Pearl.

She had rare blue eyes and a snowy white coat that no wolf in her pack had. Her pack had light grey wolves, and they had yellow eyes, but Pearl was different.

Her pack's name was sunshine. But she wasn't a member yet. Yes, her family was from the sunshine pack, but it was the rule of the pack that a wolf can't be accepted to the pack unless the young wolf hunts its first reindeer.

Until then, the wolf will not hunt with the pack, it will hunt alone for the reindeer. The wolf can't start a family, but the wolf will be invited to the meeting that's held every month, under the light of the full moon.

Pearl was trying to hunt every day, every single day; but she always failed.

The leader of the pack called Storm did give her something to eat. But today was the start of a new month, and in the yesterday's meeting Storm had told Pearl that she only had this month as a chance, which meant that she had to hunt before this month's meeting or else she will not live in the sunshine pack's territory, and she will have to live her life as a wandering wolf, with no family or friends.

And that's such a bad fate for such a beautiful wolf like Pearl.

And now with a heavy heart she went back.

Pearl was met with stares of pity. Her freind tried to encourage her while a male grey whose name was Alaska who was her rival said

"Hah! So that means you will live alone for the rest of your life!"

Pearl glared him steadily with her blue eyes and spoke

"No! I can hunt today too; a whole day is left and I have a whole month ahead of me"

Alaska narrowed his eyes at her and trotted away. The whole pack was going away to *hunt*.

Although Pearl would never say it, she secretly admired Alaska for his skills. He was actually the best hunter in the pack. And so now and then, whenever the pack would go to hunt, Pearl would sit on a rock away from the hunting ground and watch Alaska as he led the hunting team.

She was about to watch Alaska when she thought she could practice hunting on smaller mammals, like rabbits. Yes, she could hunt rabbits but for being admitted to the pack she had to hunt a reindeer.

She quickly spotted a hare eating some flowers.

When the hunting team returned, Pearl had hunted two hares and already ate them. So, when Storm gave her a piece of reindeer, she refused because she wasn't hungry.

Pearl again looked for a reindeer, she followed it, almost sprang on it, fell and got a kick on her back. She tried three times, but failed.

It was night now, and time to go to sleep. When every wolf had slept and it was past midnight. She creeped out of her den and trotted to a cliff where you could see the whole forest. And the starry sky.

But when she reached there, she saw a wolf.

The wolf was Alaska

What is he doing here?

She creeped closer and sat on the cliff, looking at the sky. Neither of them spoke until Alaska broke the silence.

"I'm sorry about the times I...erm discouraged you. I was too proud of my skills and I thought I was better than any wolf...but my father says that's not a good thing for a leader to have"

Pearl smiled to herself, Alaska was the sun of Storm, and he was to be the sunshine pack's alpha soon.

"it's alright. I don't think I'm a good wolf at all." Pearl replied.

"No, your personality isn't defined with hunting. Your personality is defined by your heart. If you are kind, then you are a good wolf." Alaska said.

Why is he so reassuring today?

Pearl asked herself.

"But if I don't hunt, I will be a lone wolf."

Pearl's blue eyes were filled with sadness

"You know how I hunt so good?"

Alaska answered his own question

"Because I have found my inner power. My power lies in my speed. And I discovered that power when I was hunting for my reindeer, for being accepted into the pack"

"Does everybody have an inner power?" asked Pearl.

"Yes Pearl. My father's power is his growl, my mother's power is her bite. You just have to discover your inner power."

Pearl nodded and asked another question

"And how will I discover it?"

Alaska smiled; Pearl did ask a lot of questions.

"I don't know, you have to try everything I suppose. Like sometimes you use speed, sometimes you use your growl, sometimes your bite, sometimes your claws, sometimes you use ambush."

Alaska stopped for a moment and continued; "Try everything, and the one which fits you is your inner power. And yeah, I can teach you how to hunt, you hunt a bit incorrectly"

So that meant Alaska watched her while she hunted.

Pearl said "Thank you so much, when will you teach me?"

Alaska replied

"Tomorrow is it"

~~~~~~~~~~~~~~~~~~~~~~~
~~~~~~~~~~~~~~~~~~~~~~~

Speed

"Can I try speed first? Or growl? Or bite? Or what?" Pearl was heaping a load of questions on Alaska who had just returned from his hunt

He replied

"Anything you wish"

"Speed then"

They both went to the hunting ground which was covered with snow, tufts of grass were growing here and there and a herd of reindeers were grazing over there.

Pearl and Alaska were hidden behind a boulder, Alaska said

"Good, now when you near the reindeer, instead of leaping on it, overtake it. When you are in front of it you can jump for the neck. That's how you hunt when you use speed."

Pearl nodded, unsure of herself. She didn't think she will be able to run that fast. But she had to try.

Alaska gave her more instructions

"You now scan the herd and see the one which will be the easiest to catch. See for a young foal, or an old reindeer or an injured one, reindeers who are away from the herd are also easy to catch"

Pearl scanned the place with her eyes the colour of the sky. She found a lucky catch, an old injured reindeer!

Alaska also saw it and spoke

"Catching this one's gonna be very easy. You can do it"

From boulder to boulder, she crept closer and closer to her prey.

Pearl came into the view and the reindeer made a dash for his life.

Pearl also ran, very fast. She was near the reindeer's legs, very nearby. She heard Alaska shout.

"AWAY FROM THE LEGS! NO!"

Pearl yelped as the reindeer kicked her and ran away.

The whole reindeer herd ran away, and Alaska came to her

"Are you alright?" he asked

Her face did hurt

"I think so, I'm sorry" she replied

"No, its alright, but being near the legs is a very big mistake, for overtaking the reindeer you have to be on its side"

Pearl didn't say anything

"We will practice on speed today, if you fail then we will move the other tactic tomorrow"

Pearl nodded

"Do some rest now"

They both walked to the den-place and Alaska went to his father, he had been called by him.

Pearl went to her den but found a proud wolf whose name was Laila sitting in *her* den. Laila said

"Hi loser! I saw you hunting like fools"

Pearl was hurt by her words but she was used to all this, she politely replied

"Oh, hi Laila, how are you? Could you go back to your den please? I'm a bit tired you know"

Laila replied crossly

"Huh loser, you are not even like wolf, why do you even have this den?"

You are not even like a wolf; you are not even like a wolf. Loser, loser.

Laila's words pierced her heart and her ears. Pearl's heart burned and she spat her words out

"What sort of wolf you are? You don't even know how to speak properly! You are just jealous of me that I'm beautiful and I hate you!"

Laila was surprised, whenever Pearl was bullied, she never spoke, and now...this.

Laila stood up and went out of the cave.

Pearl sat down, her heart thumping against her chest. She was not supposed to talk with the pack members like this, she knew she would be called to the alpha.

Laila came and declared dramatically; head held high

"The alpha seeks you"

Pearl rose with heavy steps and went to the cave. The cave that belonged to the alpha.

Alaska was also there, and Storm gazed at her. They both didn't seem angry though

Before any of them could speak, Pearl said

"She called me a loser, and said I wasn't a wolf, she was in my cave too."

"that's not why we called you dear, Laila always does that" Storm said

Pearl breathed a sigh of relief, but she thought

Then why did they call me?

Storm continued "Alaska told me about your quest to find your inner power. Every wolf is unique, and almost all of them have unique inner powers. Our inner powers depend on this" the alpha raised his paw to his heart. The alpha continued;

"Your parents named you Pearl because they wanted you to have a unique name. your mother had disagreed with the name first, but your father persuaded her. Your father was unique too, and his inner power laid in his howl. He was an amazing wolf. The aurora which lights the sky for us is a special thing. It makes you believe in yourself"

Alaska said;

"I believe in you already though"

Pearl was silent. Her father had died when she was very small. Nobody ever told her his inner power. And now she knew

"His blood runs in your veins. He was unique just like you are" Storm said

"let's go hunt"

Pearl nodded and followed Alaska out of the cave.

They were in the hunting ground and there were some reindeers busy grazing.

Pearl's eyes scanned the herd and she found the reindeer she had missed a while ago

"You are lucky Pearl, now try it. And stay away from the legs!"

Pearl creeped nearer to her prey and made a dash for it. But she failed, *again*.

Her heart was broken, she was useless and had no purpose.

"No Pearl, everything has a purpose. Don't give up."

Pearl went back to her cave, which hopefully had no intruders.

"We might see aurora today, meet me at the cliff at midnight" Alaska had said before going away to his den.

When she was going to the cliff, Pearl had seen a hint of green of the black cloak of the sky.

And that meant Aurora Borealis was coming up.

~~~~~~~~~~~~~~~~~~~~~~~~
~~~~~~~~~~~~~~~~~~~~~~~~

CHAPTER THREE

Aurora

"Every time I see it, it seems new" Pearl said, her voice full of astonishment.

Greenish-blue belts of light danced across the sky. There were no stars, but the Northen lights were beautiful even without the stars or anything.

Alaska nodded, his green eyes (he was the only one who had green eyes) shone brightly. They both seemed to prefer the silence.

Pearl found a new power, a new feeling she had never felt. Her heart thumped against her chest, and she felt excitement, to try new tactics, to find her inner power. She was special, her father was special, her appearance was unique, and her inner power would be unique too.

She started to believe in herself.

First the feeling was so small that she didn't even feel it. But it grew and grew until it filled her chest.

I will try my bite tomorrow

She thought.

The aurora had stopped, and it was still night.

Alaska said;

"So, time to hunt!"

"Right now?" Pearl asked

"Yes"

"I can try bite"

"alright"

They both went down the cliff and stalked to the hunting ground.

Alaska told her;

"Now, the reindeer will run and you have to chase it. When you get near the reindeer you bite its leg which makes it fall."

Pearl nodded, that seemed difficult but the aurora made her believe in herself.

''Now go, you can do this"

"okay"

She scanned the sleeping herd and saw the reindeer she had missed yesterday. She felt anger because it seemed that reindeer was challenging her.

"don't hunt with your anger, hunt with your mind" Alaska said, as if reading her mind.

Pearl didn't understand what he was trying to say but she knew she couldn't be angry or else everything would be wrong.

From boulder to boulder, she stalked her prey. The reindeer made a dash for his life and Pearl gave it a chase. Well, when she tried to bite the reindeer, she got kicked and the reindeer ran away, leaving Pearl panting on the snow.

~~~~~~~~~~~~~~~~~~~~~~
~~~~~~~~~~~~~~~~~~~~~~

CHAPTER FOUR

Emergency!

Alaska helped Pearl in every way he could. He gave her tips and things...but Pearl's luck was against her. She couldn't hunt a single dear. No one knows why she couldn't.

But one day, when they were coming back after excepting defeat, they heard a howl. It was a howl that meant emergency! It was coming from the alpha's den.

They both started off as a gallop. They ran like the wind.

Alaska was the first to reach the den, without giving it a moment's thought, he trotted straight in the den. While Pearl was behind him, her fur out of order completely because of the blind running. She followed Alaska's lead and went straight into the den.

Storm didn't seem to be in good shape. Almost all the wolves of the pack were gathered around him. Alaska seemed shocked, and the oldest wolf of sunshine pack named "Dark" because he was very dark grey, began in his crinkling voice;

"Storm has a rare disease which will cause him to die in a week. My father had died because of the same disease. The cure of the disease is healdeer"

Everybody listened to dark.

Dark continued;

"Healdeer live in the valley of flowers. Their meat can cure any type of illness. The flower valley is very far away from our territory. As you might know."

Every wolf nodded, except Pearl. As she was not a member of the pack yet she didn't understand what dark was trying to tell them.

Every wolf of the sunshine pack knew the way to the flower valley. It's so long it can't be mentioned over here. But hardly any wolf dared to go there, for the journey was long and dangerous.

"Two wolves have to go."

Although they loved their leader, none of them stepped forward until Alaska announced

"I will go!"

Pearl was a brave wolf. She spoke

"I can go with you if you want"

Alaska knew no one like he knew Pearl. He knew Pearl never gave up, and she was his true friend.

"You will go with me" Alaska said, nodding at Pearl.

Laila was taken aback, a wolf who can't even hunt is chosen by Alaska?

Before Laila could say anything, Storm pushed his words out

"Pearl...will...go...with...Alaska...wish...you...a...safe...journey."

Dark nodded, and Alaska told all the wolves to go out of the cave. His father needed a rest.

It wasn't like Storm was very old. He was fit and active, he could lead the pack. But it was a rule that when a son of an alpha reaches a particular age, the son becomes the alpha. The disease Storm had caught wasn't because of old age, it could happen to anybody.

Every wolf in the pack had developed a new respect for Pearl and Alaska. They had shown incredible bravery in agreeing to go. Yes, for the journey to the flower valley is far from easy, one has to climb mountains, face snow storms...and there are lots of polar bears on the way, and healdeer are not easy to hunt.

"We don't have time; we leave tomorrow by dusk." Said Alaska

"I suppose you all must hunt so we can prepare?" Pearl said to the wolves circled around her.

They all nodded and followed Alaska. The wolves had seen Pearl was loyal as any other wolf, it didn't matter to them that Pearl wasn't a pack member at all.

~~~~~~~~~~~~~~~~~~~~~~~~~~
~~~~~~~~~~~~~~~~~~~~~~~~~~

CHAPTER FIVE

Moonlight Pack

"Come after 6 days!"

"Look out for the polar bears!"

"Stop in a snow Storm!"

"Climb the mountain carefully!"

"You rememeber the way, right?"

Every wolf of the pack was concerned about Pearl and Alaska. They both had eaten and said their goodbyes to Storm.

Pearl swallowed, looking at the end of the hunting field. There would be no protection out there, just a vast, endless landscape of white snow. BUT, Pearl would do it, for Alaska, for Storm, and this was the chance to prove herself, and find her inner power.

Alaska ruffled his fur. He was ready, *always* ready for the adventure ahead of them, he has his friend by his side. What else could he need?

Storm was getting weaker and weaker, there was no time to lose.

As the sky was dark blue, and the sun started to rise. Alaska announced

"Time for me and Pearl to go"

All the wolves nodded, and they all saw them, going and going until they disappeared out of sight.

"Are you ready to howl the permission howl?"

Alaska said. Pearl knew permission howl was a howl that was howled when they had to cross other pack's territory. Pearl asked;

"What wolf pack's territory is this?"

"The moonlight pack, our rivals. Their territory is very long and the wolves of the moonlight pack are dark coloured, they want our territory too. When my father was young our pack had fought with these wolves" Alaska replied

"So, we have to cross their pack's territory, are you sure they won't harm us?" Pearl asked again

"Well, the wolf law says not to harm a passer-by, but to tell the truth moonlight pack have always been law breakers." He replied, thinking his knowledge come to use.

"Don't you have another route?" Pearl further asked

"No, you will howl" Alaska told Pearl, thinking she also needed a chance to do something.

Pearl obeyed his orders and sat on her haunches. She raised her head, her nose pointing to the sky, and howled.

The howl was good, loud and clear. The moonlight pack must've easily heard that. And as Pearl had started, she stopped, for they both had seen a dark figure coming towards them.

The wolf was a male, with dark grey fur and the chest had light grey fur. His eyes were yellow, and had an evil expression. With one ear was twisted he had scars on his face.

Some other wolves followed. And the first one sneered

"Asking for permission, are we?"

"Yes, and I-we will be glad if you let us pass through" Alaska said protectively, not wanting a fight.

Pearl backed away behind Alaska, she wanted to say something, but she was *scared*.

The wolf again said

"Hah! My name is scar, and it's not easy to pass our territory. You have to fight me, if you win you pass, if you don't win...well we think what to do next."

"But that's not the wolf law!" Alaska growled, knowing where the conversation was heading.

The other wolves behind him smiled, including Scar, he said; "But that's our law, if you don't want you, or your friend get harmed, fight or get ready"

Scar was looking at Pearl that made her growl. Her fur was bristled and she was ready to fight. Alasa said;

"No, you are not fighting Pearl. It's between Scar and me."

Pearl whispered;

"You will win"

Alaska nodded thankfully and Pearl sat at a safe distance on her haunches to watch the fight.

Alaska took a step towards Scar. So did he.

They were both very close, and then they circled each other, growling. Their tails waving with their teeth bared. Alaska tried biting Scar's tail, but Scar pounced away, and then jumped at Alaska at full speed to pin him down, but Alaska was not a fool. He was quick and intelligent.

Alaska darted sideways sending Scar crashing on the snow, it took some moments for him to be on his feet again.

Alaska decided to strike, he growled and Scar's side. Scar bit back. Pearl gasped. None of the wolves were wanting to leave their bite. Pearl shouted;

"DEFEND"

Alaska got the clue and left his grip, bit his claws scratched Scar's face, which made Scar lose his grip on

Alaska's ears too.

Both of the wolves backed away and started circling each other again, Scar tried biting Alaska's tail and Alaska pounced on Scar, ready to pin him down. But Scar caught Alaska's paw on mid-flight causing Alaska to lose his balance and falling to the ground. Pearl gasped again and spoke

"STRIKE"

But Scar had almost pinned Alaska down, and that meant Scar would win if he put both his forepaws on Alaska.

"DO THE SAME!" Pearl shouted

Alaska had almost given up, but hearing Pearl's voice surged power in him.

He was not alone.

~~~~~~~~~~~~~~~~~~~~~~~~
~~~~~~~~~~~~~~~~~~~~~~~~

Snowstorm

Alaska dug his teeth into Scar's forepaw, he jerked his paws away, howling in pain.

When Alaska did loosen his grip on Scar's paw, he shot up and jumped on Scar, taking Scar down by surprise and pinning him to the ground, putting one of his forepaws on Scar's throat to make sure he didn't escape.

Pearl gave a howl of victory, the other wolves of the moonlight pack grumbled. The alpha came and spoke

"You have defeated my son; he will soon become an alpha and thereby seek his revenge"

Alaska growled back

"I will become an alpha soon too, and we shall fight again."

Scar snarled at Alaska and went away. The alpha leaded Pearl and Alaska out of there territory. When they were finally out, the alpha stopped and turned back. And both of the wolves ran until they were away from the territory.

"Thank you...for encouraging me"

Pearl replied

"I didn't think that would have made a difference...I was just myself"

"Well, it did make a difference, if you hadn't told me to do the same, I would have lost"

Pearl blushed; they walked in silence for a while until;

"Your howls were quite special; I had never heard a howl like that."

"Thank you, I never thought of it like that." Pearl thanked him

"Remember what the alpha told you? That your father's blood runs in your veins."

Pearl did remember, but she said nothing.

Alaska caught Pearl glancing upwards in the sky anxiously, he asked her;

"Whats up?"

"I don't know, but-but I think a snow-Storm's coming up"

Alaska's heart skipped a beat, they had to find a shelter- and quick!

"Follow me, I can see some glaciers from here, perhaps we can find some shelter there"

They both ran to the glaciers, if Pearl hadn't been in hurry, she might have stopped to see the beauty of them.

The glacier was almost a very light blue, they towered above Pearl and Alaska, the glacier was high and simply *magnificent*.

"Sometimes there are holes in the glaciers, we can hide in there" Alaska said urgently.

They circled every glacier and still couldn't find a place to hide. The wind was starting to build up.

"HIDE BEHIND THE GLACIER!" Alaska shouted, for the snow Storm had truly begin

"THAT WILL BE NO USE! WE MUST STIILL KEEP LOOKING!" Pearl shouted back.

The snow was mixed up with wind, and the wind was freezingly, bitterly cold. It made Pearl and Alaska shiver. The snow got in their eyes, covered their noses, and shattered their ears.

But still...

...they couldn't give up...

...so, they circled every glacier.

"WE...will...freeze...to death." Alaska gasped

But Pearl wasn't the giving up kind. She spoke

"You stay here...I'm looking for a hole, there must be one here"

Pearl whispered into his ear. Alaska didn't reply, his strengths were failing him, he curled into a ball and closed his eyes.

Pearl had to find a shelter or else Alaska and she would die.

Pearl didn't care how fast the wind was, she ran, circled the glaciers and sniffed every part, every part she could look at, she found a hole, small but enough for both of them.

She ran back to where she had found Alaska, but instead there was blood.

Blood?

She heard a roar; it didn't belong to the Storm.

It was a polar bear's roar.

~~~~~~~~~~~~~~~~~~~~~
~~~~~~~~~~~~~~~~~~~~~

CHAPTER SEVEN

Fight Or Flight?

The snow Storm had lessened, but it was still cold. Pearl couldn't see anything but she knew something bad has happened to Alaska. She could have hidden in the hole but she couldn't just leave Alaska behind.

Wolves will die for their pack.

And that's what Pearl would do.

When the polar bear roared, Pearl howled.

She howled at polar bear, she howled for Alaska, she howled for Storm, she howled for herself. Her anger, her pain, her sadness all in one howl. Her howl was loud and clear.

The polar bear came into view, and Pearl growled

"Don't you dare come any further!"

"Aye, don't ya worry, that wolf is safe an' sound, a polar bear tried to kill that wolf, but he's safe now."

The polar bear said. It was a female.

She had tufts of white fur like snow on her head and back, but mostly was a very light yellow. Her ears were shaped like soft triangles and kept like fragile things on her head, and a black nose which seemed moist and healthy.

Pearl had personally never met a polar bear, she had been so busy in hunting that she couldn't enjoy...life, this colour and adventures.

Pearl edged a little closer to the bear and asked

"Who are you? And how is Alaska? And how can I trust you?"

Her voice was low but clear, the bear might not have heard her as the snow Storm was still there. Pearl repeated her questions, then the bear replied

"My name is Snowpaw, and is Alaska the name of the wolf? Well, if yes then he is doing well and is in my den, safe but maybe not that cosy, and well I don't know how to prove that you can trust me, but I assure you I don't eat wolves, only seals and I already ate before the Storm."

Pearl liked the honesty of Snowpaw, her voice had a tone which told Pearl that she could trust the polar bear, it was like a sixth sense Pearl had.

"Take me to Alaska, will you?" Pearl said

Snowpaw nodded and told Pearl too follow her. They walked past 4 glaciers and finally came to a halt. Snowpaw looked around and went around the glacier, stopping at a beautiful den-shaped hole carved inside the glacier

"This is my home"

Pearl was awe-stricken, she had never seen anything like that. But Pearl was tired, her bones felt like Jelly. She wanted a rest; it was night and the snow Storm was still fast and strong.

"Come in" Snowpaw told Pearl.

Pearl followed her into the cave, she heard rasp short breaths then a growl.

"Pearl! Is this you?" Alaska said, surprised

Pearl nodded "Yes Alaska, me, are you alright?"

Alaska nodded then realized that there was a polar bear, he gave a growl

"Don't worry, she saved you, I found a little cave we can spend the night in"

Pearl said, reassuring Alaska.

Snowpaw nodded and spoke

"Can you tell me more about yourself tomorrow? I would like to help you all"

This time Alaska said

"Thank you, we can talk about this"

Pearl led Alaska to the cave and they both just fitted fine in there, Alaska told Pearl

"You showed a lot of bravery today, Pearl, and you didn't give up, you will make a great leader, maybe even better than me."

And with that they both slept deeply

They had reached the glaciers and the polar bears, the first landmark of their journey.

~~~~~~~~~~~~~~~~~~~~~~~
~~~~~~~~~~~~~~~~~~~~~~~

Journey

"You are really hurt, dude" Snowpaw says to Alaska the morning after the snowstorm, nodding at his bloody front paw

"Yeah...the polar bear wounded me...a bit" Alaska replies licking his wounds

"They are not very seriuse, but I am worried how we will continue the journey, it's a long way to flower valley" Pearl said sadly.

"Hey! Did you just say...flower valley?!" Snowpaw stares at them, shocked out of her mind

"Well yeah...." And so, Pearl tells from the beginning, about the sunlight pack, her not being able to hunt, and then the sickness of Storm, and the fight between Alaska and Scar, and how they got trapped in the snowstorm.

"...and that's how we met you!" Pearl finished
Snowpaw was pacing from there to here, she said
"You both are brave and have passed some challenges, but..."
She stopped at but, looking at Alaska and Pearl with her big sad eyes
"But what?" Alaska asked
"Many wolves came here, asking for directions to the flower valley, they go, sometimes come without

anything....and sometimes never return"

"What stops them? Why do some never return?" Pearl asked jumping to her feet, urging Snowpaw to tell them more

"Humans, *homo sapiens*, men, hunters, people" Snowpaw said

Humans? Pearl and Alaska had heard about them, but they never thought they would meet one!

"You are...joking" Alaska said, startled

"Not all are bad, I know some humans who can heal Alaska's paw" Snowpaw told.

"Are you sure?" Pearl asked

"Yep, they helped me once when I got hurt in a fight, I didn't bite them once I learned they were helping me, and I know where they live! Just a little further from the glaciers, they are very nice, don't worry" Snowpaw explained

"I think we must eat something before going there" Alaska said

"As we are near the sea, lots of seals are avalable, can hunt some for you." Snowpaw offered

"I can help" Alaska said, and got up but winced at the pain of his paw

"Hunting won't help your paw Alaska, its gonna get it worse" Pearl exclaimed

"I agree with Pearl, but you better stay with me, you both are not safe without me" Snowpaw told them

The wolves nodded and followed Snowpaw.

"The ice's melting so not much food is avalable these days" Snowpaw exclaims sadly, gazing at the empty shores.

"That's what my pack's been noticing from some time, not much seals and walruses are avalable these days, so we stick to the reindeer and musk oxen" Alaska adds

"You guys are lucky, hunting reindeer is very difficult, they run waayyy too fast" Snowpaw said.

Pearl didn't know about this, she wished she was the part of the sunshine pack, she liked knowing facts like these, she asked; "Why are seals disappearing?"

Snowpaw answers; "Because ice's melting"

"Why is ice melting?" Pearl questioned again

"Because water is getting warmer than it should" this time, Alaska answers.

"And why is that?" Pearl didn't mean to annoy her friends, she was just curious

"Because of humans!" Snowpaw answered, impatiently

Alaska shook his head and explained: "Well, humans are warming this world, and I don't know how...but they are"

"That's bad" Pearl said

And they all agreed.

~~~~~~~~~~~~~~~~~~~~~~~~~~~
~~~~~~~~~~~~~~~~~~~~~~~~~~~

CHAPTER NINE

Humans

"So, are you ready to go wolves?" Snowpaw asked them after they were done eating a seal they had found with some difficulty (hunting it wasn't really a difficult thing for polar bears can kill a seal with a one swipe of their paw).

"Yup" Pearl agrees

"I'm ready, where are we going btw?" Alaska says

"To those nice people, to treat your paw" Snowpaw answer

"Uh, are you sure there are no...hunters over there huh?" Pearl asks, as always

"it's not like I have been there a lot of times, I have been there only one time and I have not seen many people over there" Snowpaw answers

Alaska says; "which direction?"

"North, follow the sea's coast with the mountains in front of you." Snowpaw explains

"That's exactly our route to the flower valley" Alaska observes.

Pearl nods and then they all start their journey.

Pearl marvelled at the views, glaciers where quite far away but they seemed very lovely from far, they shined in the sunlight like a star.

The mountains where far too but they were also very beautiful, they seemed majestic, towering above everything surrounding. They were grey, like Alaska's fur.

Then Alaska started running, he said to all of them

"Want to race?"

"Go for it!" Snowpaw agrees

Pearl smiled, but she knew she wouldn't win because Alaska was fast, but it sounded fun.

Snowpaw took the lead in the starting, but seemed surprised when Alaska overtook her, Pearl shouted from behind

"Arctic wolves can run 46 kmph, don't look so surprised! And Alaska is the fastest of our wolf pack!"

"You seem fast too." Snowpaw replied when Pearl was level with her.

"I didn't know that! Thanks!"

And with that, Pearl overtook her and was behind Alaska.

"Stop! The cabins are in front of us!" Snowpaw commended

The wolves slowly came to a halt and peered curiously at the red cabins.

"We have to be careful, can any of you howl to grab the human's attention?" Snowpaw asked

"Are you sure they will help?" Alaska asked, cautiously looking at the cabins.

"I'm sure, almost" Snowpaw whispered.

"Pearl, we will both howl"

Pearl nodded and raised her head, Alaska did the same and they both howled, their deep calls echoing through the vast tundra.

The red cabin door creaked open, and out of it came out a lady, she looked clearly very shocked in seeing the wolves.

But when she looked at Alaska's paw she went back inside.

Snowpaw wasn't there.

"Where are you Snowpaw?" Pearl said, looking around

"I'm hiding, if they see me, they are gonna get alarmed and might hurt us, so good luck, I'm going!"

Alaska shook his head.

The lady came out and smiled at both of the wolves, one grey and one white, with beautiful soft fur and pretty eyes. They seemed like a piar.

"Oh my god! The white one has blue eyes!" a boy which came from behind the lady said.

Some people came out and where admiring Pearl and Alaska, the lady who seemed to be in charge said

"The grey one seems wounded in the paw; it could get septic"

All other agreed. One slowly came nearer to the wolves and said softly to the other people behind her

"I have got this! Don't you worry!"

She came slowly and slowly forward, stopping, then again moving. Pearl stepped a little back and the girl stopped again. Alaska watched her attentively; he didn't even seem to be blinking.

The girl was very close to Pearl, she said as softly as she could, to both of them

"Now stay still pretties, I will just put some cream on your paw"

Alaska didn't move, he now trusted her.

The girl slowly reached to her pocket and spoke

"My name is Aurora, and I take care of wolves, they trust me, the wound seemed to be caused by a polar bear"

Aurora took out a tube and slowly took Alaska's wounded paw in her hands, grasping it firmly but gently. First, she wiped his paw clean with cottonwool then putted some antiseptic cream to ward of infections.

"Oh well! Here you go, all good." Aurora says smiling a-too-bright-smile.

She stroked Pearl's head and a person came with some meat. Pearl ate some of it while Alaska kept guard, not eating.

Aurora was fascinated by Pearl, a pure white wolf with blue eyes (blue eyes are actually 'almost' impossible in adult wolves, only wolf pups has them when they are born and then it changes colour when the pup grows up)

And on top of that, Pearl was the friendliest wolf aurora had ever met.

Aurora was very special, when a wild wolf was injured, she could help it without any problems, the wolf would sit peacefully like a loyal dog and let aurora do whatever she wanted (which was always treating wounds).

Alaska got up when he felt better, he looked around to see where is their direction to the flower valley.

He saw the mountains and the shore, they had to keep the coastline at their right and the mountains in front of them until they reached the mountains.

"Pearl, we have to go" Alaska told her.

Pearl nodded and got up, aurora understood they were going, she whispered to both.

"There are hunters in this area, do you mind if I follow you to keep you safe?"

Pearl nodded, there was no way she could say yes. Alaska flicked his ears hoping she'd take it as a yes.

"So, I can follow you? Great! When you will be safe, I will leave you both."

That was acceptable.

With the wolves' snouts pointed to the north, and aurora with her skis, they were ready to go.

If only they knew what was going to happen.

CHAPTER TEN

Captured

A big truck stops in front of them, spraying snow on Alaska.

He snarled, placing himself in front of Pearl and Aurora.

Wolves are like that, highly defensive of their family and friends.

Aurora gasped and mouthed "Hunters"

She came in front with the wolves by her heals, the truck door opened and the person who came out of it smiled a wicked sort of smile, he said;

"Aurora don't do this again, hand me over the wolves"

"Or what will you do?"

Aurora was defensive now, no way she was going to hand them her wolves, they always did that.

"Then I will take the wolves by force"

Aurora shook her head and clicked her tongue

"You are never able to take any wolves from me"

"But now we will" the hunter said

He had a Scar above his right eyebrow and he wore a brown outfit, bad for camouflage if he was to live in the snow.

Pearl growled; Alaska snarled.

The hunter was joined by two more people, one of them had a gun like thing in his hand, and then he pointed it at Alaska and shot.

Alaska gave a short bark and jumped sideways.

It was a net that could capture, they always used it for hunting arctic foxes, and now it will be used for artic wolves.

Aurora whispered to both of them

"Run and follow me at my signal"

When the hunter took the net-gun to have a go at Pearl, Aurora shouted

"NOW!"

She ran as fast as lighting towards a cliff, with the wolves following her, they were also fast as lightning.

The hunters, seening there was no chance in out running them, took out a gun, they tried to point it at Alaska, but it was impossible because they were moving too much.

The leader of the hunters said: "Zack, Tony, get the truck it's our only chance"

Zack and Tony were the names of his helpers, his name was Rio.

They all boarded at the truck and looked around for the wolves and Aurora, but they were nowhere to be seen.

"Maybe they are behind the cliff" Zack suggested

"let's look" Rio agreed

Tony nodded and turned the truck towards the cliff.

"Where is your pack?" Aurora asked the wolves

Well, they were very far from their pack.

Alaska felt very helpless, he had to heal his father, and rule the pack. And now they needed their pack, but there was no way their pack could come.

"You both are alone?" Aurora asked.

Pearl howled the permission howl; a wolf territory had its boundary just here. They could ask for help from the wolves that came out.

"What. Are. You. Doing" Alaska snapped

"Asking for help" Pearl answered as a matter-of-fact

"A wolf territory nearby?" Alaska asked, trying to piece it togather

"You didn't sense it?" Pearl asked

"Geuss I didnt"

Aurora was alarmed, she couldn't understand the wolf language ofcourse, so to human ears Alaska's and Pearl's talks sounded just like a series of growls, and a howl?

Pearl's plan worked, some light grey wolves came

"Need help?" they asked, not looking surprised by the fact that Aurora (because she had helped the pack several times), a human being was in front of them.

"how'd you know?" Alaska asked

"We heard the commotion"

"We will jump on them once they try to capture you" Another wolf said

"Thank you"

"We do that a lot, those hunters are lame, nothing to be afraid of"

Aurora thought this wolf pack was Alaska's and Pearl's, so she was calm.

A sound of brakes came behind the cliff, the wolves covered and stalked. The door was banged shut and then a sound of shot rang through the tundra

"THEY ARE HERE!" tony shouted

"Aye, found you...what?" Rio said when he saw the other wolves.

The wolves growled, including Pearl and Alaska

"Where did you get the other wolves?" Zack asked

"They came by them self" aurora replied.

The other pack wolves growled again, louder this time. Pearl howled, and howled. Alaska took the cue and howled too.

The hunters were visibly surprised, Rio shook his head and tried to point his net gun at Pearl. But then the wolves attacked and took him down, Zack and Tony scampered to the truck. The window opened a bit.

Rio was a bit wounded, a small scratch on his hand, the wolves didn't harm him that much willingly, they didn't want to be seen as bad animals. The wolves left him and he ran to the truck too.

Aurora was stuck to the cliff, surprised. Thinking that the truck would go now, but it didn't. instead, the window opened more and boom!

Pearl was entangled in a net; she had tried to dodge the net but to no avail. Alaska growled furiously and tried to bite the net off. Rio came out with a gun in his hand and exclaimed

"If anyone tries to attack me, they are gone"

~~~~~~~~~~~~~~~~~~~~~~
~~~~~~~~~~~~~~~~~~~~~~

CHAPTER ELEVEN

Captured Again

"Please, go away, why do want to hunt everything?" Aurora said, feeling helpless.

The other wolves backed away, and whispered to Alaska;

"We have to go; we tried our best but we will not risk our lives for wolves we barely even know"

"I understand, thank you, good hunting to you all" Alaska replied.

"Safe journey to you" the other pack said and went away.

"The other wolves have gone, now what?" Rio said, smirking.

"I don't know, but leave her alone" Aurora said

"Nah, it's a long time we had such a pretty wolf for our catch" Tony spoke, joining Rio.

"a beautiful wolf like her deserves to live her life in the snow, not getting killed" Aurora said.

"She's not getting killed, not by us anyway, a person wanted a white wolf alive, she's gonna fetch a lot of money." Zack explained

"But they're gonna jail her, every wolf deserves to be free!" Aurora protested.

"And we need money, shut up or else we are gonna capture the other wolf-the grey one-too" Rio threatened.

But Alaska didn't back up and snarled. Pearl stopped struggling, not wanting Alaska to help her so he wouldn't be captured too.

Aurora shook her head and came over to Alaska, who was sitting on his hunches and looking broken. She grabbed him by the scruff and took him behind, she also didn't want Alaska to be captured, she whispered to him;

"Don't worry grey, we will help your friend"

Tony and Zack were dragging the net to the back of the truck which had the door opened by Rio, the dragging of the net didn't harm Pearl. Alaska howled with anger; Pearl howled back.

Aurora watched as Rio closed the truck garage door which had Pearl inside, aurora gave the hunters an angry look, it looked like she would growl, but she didn't.

The hunters went inside the truck to their driver seats and drove off, leaving Aurora and Alaska alone.

Alaska had to go to the flower valley to save his father, he had to return to his pack, to lead them. But he needed a companion during this journey, and his companion was gone.

NO! that's when Alaska thought he could try to do something, everybody was counting on him, he licked aurora's hands and ran behind the truck.

"NO! grey stop! We will think of something else!" Aurora shouted.

But Alaska won't listen, why must he when he was the alpha of such a big pack? He had to save a very good friend and nothing could stop him.

The hunters hadn't seen Alaska following, so they were driving the truck on their own pace. They were quite far from aurora; she couldn't be seen.

Alaska was very tired of all the running, the truck stopped for a break, and Alaska stopped with it too.

When tony came out, Alaska gave him a surprise attack. Pinning him down and standing on his hands so he couldn't get up. Then Alaska growled but tony was still as snow.

Rio saw all the drama and banged his flare gun which made Alaska to jump back, and then Zack captured him too with a net.

"So, he came too, is Aurora anywhere here?" Rio asked

"I don't think so" Tony told.

"Are you wounded?" Zack asked tony.

"No, surprisingly" Tony replied.

Alaska was snarling and growling and barking, trying to bite the net off.

The hunters dragged him to the truck garage, opened the door very slightly, opened the net a little and heaved him inside. Then they started to drive the truck.

"Why did you come?" Pearl asked Alaska when he had struggled out of his net.

"For you" Alaska answered.

"Thanks. But now none of us can go to the flower valley because we are captured."

"We are wolves, we live togather. I miss my pack; I cannot travel alone so if you were not with me, I would've gone back"

"So now what?"

"Escape from this...place. And attack the hunters too, and bite them"

"*The only thing that's worse than our claw's our bite*" Pearl sings a verse of a song the wolves used to sing at the full moon meeting.

"*Oh, we own what we own, we own the might*" Alaska sings the other verse

"It was a nice song" Pearl says.
~~~~~~~~~~~~~~~~~~~~~~~~~~
~~~~~~~~~~~~~~~~~~~~~~~~~~

CHAPTER TWELVE

Escape

"So first we try to find where they are taking us" Alaska said after a while

"Don't think that'll be too difficult!" Pearl exclaims, jumping to her feet.

She went to a small hole, almost like a window on the truck's side covered with wire mesh to avoid escapes but letting the air to come inside, Pearl peeked through it and saw that the mountains were quite close.

"Come! See this!" Pearl tells Alaska excitedly.

Alaska peeks through it, feeling the air on his face. He was surprised, the truck was taking them to the mountains which had the flower valley, reaching the mountains would take a whole day, and they reached here in just a half of it! He told Pearl.

"That's great! We just have to find a way to get out from here" Pearl says, excitedly

"I see some sort of station a little up on the mountain which has the flower valley, I suppose they are gonna stop there, maybe give us some food? Anyways, we will just make a dash for the door, bite whoever tries to stop us and hide behind some rocks" Alaska made a plan.

"Great plan Alaska, I'm sure you would make a great alpha"

Alaska waves the compliment away and sits near the small wire mesh window, looking towards the station and willing it'll come soon.

The truck came to a halt and it jolted badly

"They are driving like we are being chased by mad bulls" Pearl mutters.

"No time for that, we have to carry our plans" Alaska says, hearing her.

The wolves see the hunters coming out of the truck, some other people came from the cabin and they were talking. Alaska and Pearl crouch near the truck door, ready to pounce for they had seen Tony and Zack coming towards the truck door with some meat in their hands.

The truck door rattled and it opened a little bit, Alaska jumped on the truck door, forcing it open and Pearl followed him.

They both heard some bangs, they dodged nets and they finally reached some cliffs and fallen rocks, they hid behind them.

The hunters came running, panting and swearing.

They looked around, but as there were many cliffs and rocks, they couldn't find them.

They were safe, they had escaped.

~~~~~~~~~~~~~~~~~
~~~~~~~~~~~~~~~~~

CHAPTER THIRTEEN

Singing

When the hunters were gone, Alaska climbed on a high cliff to take a good look around.

"We are on the right track; we have to go towards the north"

"I think we are completing this journey earlier, like we reached here in two days!" Pearl observes

"You are right, but we are not completing the journey, we have to go back too. And we might not get a ride in a truck"

Pearl nods as they climb higher.

There is a song that belongs to the wolves, they sing it on travels and in the moon-meetings. Alaska started singing the first paragraph

"No one's catching me unless I wanna be caught.
I'm dancing in the shadows there's no leash when I walk,
Our freedom isn't up to them it's only up to us,
I'm the alpha, I'm the leader, I'm the one to trust.
Togather we do whatever it takes, we're in this pack for life,
We're the wolves and we own the might"

Pearl listened and began on the next paragraph

"Oh, we own what we own, oh, we own the might.
The only thing's that's worse than our claw's our bite,
Oh, we own what we own, we own the might"

Alaska then began on the third

"I'm picking up the scent, it seems we are on the right track.
The moonlight's on our heads, the wind's on our backs,
We live in the snow, we're living for the chase,
Our heritage is in our sights so let's pick up the pace."

It was a good travelling paragraph.

Pearl then sings the next paragraph,

"Oh, we own what we own, oh, we own the might.
The only thing's that's worse than our claw's our bite,
Oh, we own what we own, we own the might"

Alaska then sings the next paragraph

"We're on a quest to find the power that's inside of us
I'm the Alpha, I'm the leader, I'm the one to trust.
Together we do whatever it takes, we're in this pack for life.
We're the wolves and we own the might"

Pearl then sings the last paragraph

"We own what we own,
The snow is our home,
We own what we own,
We own the might!"

And then they both complete it with a howl

"That was fun!" Alaska remarks.

"Oh yeah, it was" Pearl agrees.

It was almost night, but they kept walking. They had enough rest today and would only stop at midnight, and they had no trouble walking as wolves' eyes work perfectly in the dark.

"Do you want to sing again?" Alaska asks.

"Sure!" Pearl agrees.

They sing again, keeping sure they were on the right track.

Everything was going smoothly for now....

...for now.

SIDRA KHAN

~~~~~~~~~~~~~~~~~~~~~~
~~~~~~~~~~~~~~~~~~~~~~

CHAPTER FOURTEEN

Landslide

It was midnight and they had almost reached the peak.

"Let's find somewhere safe to sleep" Pearl suggests.

Alaska nods and they set of nosing about in rocks, trying to find a safe place.

"Hey! See I found a small den!" Alaska calls

It was a nice den; it didn't seem anything owned the den so they slept in it.

The next morning Pearl hunted some rabbits which looked like the only hunt avalable. There was a small pond which was not frozen so they drank from it.

Both of them were completely ready and they could even see a speck of green far away!

But in order to reach the valley, they had to go down the mountains from the other side, it was very dangourous. Loose rocks were all around and one wrong step could make a landslide and bury you.

And that's what happened.

Pearl kind of tripped and came down a cascade of rocks upon them, they dodged the rocks but in order to do that, they got lost.

They got separated.

When it was safe Pearl tried to find her way back, but she couldn't even see the green speck anymore.

"Alaska? Hello? Is anyone here? I'm lost" she called.

Pearl tried not to panic; an alone wolf is nothing. She heard a howl, she howled back.

But then she realized that the howl didn't belong to Alaska.

It belonged to somebody else.

Alaska looked around, everywhere he could see for Pearl, but he found her nowhere.

What am I going to do in the middle of nowhere?

He thought, sitting on a rock, he tried to think of what to do.

But for the first time he had no plan.

"Who...Are you?" Pearl shouted, gazing at a wolf-like figure which seemed to be moving towards her.

"I'm a wolf, I think you knew" the figure said once he reached her

"No...I mean whats your name?" Pearl asked, annoyed

"My name is wander, I'm from the pack adventurers and I heard you" Wander explains

"Oh well, will you help me reach the flower valley and find my friend?"

"Come with me" Wander says

Pearl hesitated then followed him, leading her to a less rocky landscape, there were some more wolves there. they had fur of all types of colours, white, dark grey, light grey, brown and some had all the colours.

"We heard your howls" A white wolf told Pearl.

"Could you lead me to the path of the flower valley?" Pearl asked for the second time.

"That's what we do" The white wolf replied

"What do you mean?" Pearl asked

"Come, let's find your friend first" the white wolf suggested, not answering her question.

The pack adventurer set of sniffing there and here, Pearl howled occasionally, to let Alaska know she was safe and so he could howl back.

The place where Pearl had ended wasn't like the valley-side of the mountain, this side wasn't sunny or cheery. It was gloomy and dark and had veils of mists. Gravel crunched beneath the wolves' paws. Some baches of snow were here and there, some groups of grass also grew.

The wolves were silent, until they heard a howl.

"Oh no, the sound of the howl is coming from the most dangourous part of this mountain; the slope" Wander exclaimed.

"The howl belongs to Alaska" Pearl observed, and to reassure him she howled back.

Alaska howled back.

"Are you alright?" Pearl shouted

"I'M STUCK!" Alaska shouted back.

"WE'RE COMING, HANG ON!" wander howled

"I'M ALREADY HANGING ON"

"3 of us wolves will go, you, wander and me" the white wolf said

"Alright, but who are you?" Pearl asked

"My name is frost, and I'm the alpha of this pack" the white wolf answered.

"Is the slope Alaska's stuck on the track to the flower valley?" Pearl asked for more info

"No, the slope to the flower valley is the other part" Frost explained.

"let's go now" Wander said

And the three wolves carefully descend down the slope.

~~~~~~~~~~~~~~~~~~~~~~
~~~~~~~~~~~~~~~~~~~~~~

CHAPTER FIFTEEN

Found

Under a pile of rocks came a howl.

"Alaska!" Pearl gasped, startled

"You are safe" Wander sighed

"Who are you?" Alaska asked, referring the wander and frost

"We're here to save you, don't worry, they're nice" Pearl reassured.

"Get me out of here then"

"alright"

So, the wolves set out nosing about the pile rocks, trying to find a point they could move a rock without the rest of the rocks crushing Alaska.

Pearl dug out the gravel from the rocks and wander helped her.

Some rocks tumbled out and Alaska jumped out.

"Fast, let's get out of this place" frost orders.

Alaska remembered how nice its was to be an alpha, he missed his pack so very much.

"I'm so happy you're safe!" Pearl boomed

"Me too" Alaska replied.

Frost leads them away to a brighter place; it wasn't very gloomy and had sunshine.

"We live here" Frost exclaimed.

Some more wolves greeted them, frost gave Pearl and Alaska something to eat.

After the introductions were done, frost told Pearl and Alaska about his pack.

The pack adventurer was a pack which had lone wolves- the wolves which were rejected by their packs because they couldn't hunt- It was a small pack, and they lived in the mountain, they usually ate rabbits. And when a wolf would come here, seeking the healdeer, this pack would lead the wolf to the valley.

There was a short-cut from the valley to the place where most of the wolf territories were found, the short-cut could only be taken from the flower to the wolf territories, not from the wolf territories to the flower valley.

Why did no one tell them about this pack? Alaska had asked, to which frost replied that no wolf who met them would not tell the other wolves about this pack or the shortcut, the pack wanted to stay secret. Alaska and Pearl were to do so if they wanted the pack to help them. So, they both promised not to tell anybody about the pack.

"So, when will you take us; to the flower valley I mean" Alaska asked

"After sometime; after a rest" Frost replied.

~~~~~~~~~~~~~~~~~~~~~
~~~~~~~~~~~~~~~~~~~~~

CHAPTER SIXTEEN

The Flower Valley

"So, let's go" frost exclaimed

Wander, frost, Pearl and Alaska were going to the flower valley. The other wolves would wait for their alpha and were to stay in their territory.

Pearl and Alaska had told frost and his pack all about their adventure, the fight between Scar and Alaska, the snowstorm, Snowpaw, good humans, being captured by hunters, escaping and the landslide.

The wolves were very fair on their paws. Frost and wander were definitely better than Alaska and Pearl at descending down the mountain, with the careful guidance of frost, Alaska and Pearl reached the flower valley.

True to its name, the flower valley was like a grassland with lots of grass and some flowers, the healdeer grazed here and there.

"Do you want to listen to a story?" Wander asks

"sure" Alaska replied.

And so, after they found a nice place behind some bushes, frost started the story.

Once upon a time, there was a wolf named wonder. He was curious about everything you can imagine. His fur was a light grey and his eyes were yellow, and they always glinted with curiosity.

Wonder was a lone wolf, he managed to survive in the vast tundra of the arctic. Day-by-day, he learnt to survive alone.

But wonder wanted to prove his pack that he was something, he found the rule of the hunting of the reindeer very unfair. He used to believe that sooner or later a wolf will learn to hunt when it finds its inner power.

So as to prove himself, he embarked on an adventure to find something unique, something that'll make him known.

Wonder crossed glaciers, the polar bears, survived landslides and the worst snowstorms. He climbed a mountain and saw a green speck.

Wonder walked day and night, towards that green speck. The green speck became bigger and bigger until he reached the place.

Wonder howled with happiness; he saw a strange sort of reindeer. Being seized with hunger, wander hunted his first ever reindeer.

Now he had found something unique, something to prove that he wasn't useless. Wrapping up a portion of the reindeer he had hunted with a leaf, he embarked on a journey to return to his pack.

He found a shortcut and used it. after reached his pack's territory, wonder was surprised with a terrible news, the alpha of his pack was sized with a terrible sickness that won't go!

The wolves of his pack were surprised to see him, but they let him stay. Wonder told all his wolf mates about his journey. Some believed him, some didn't.

Wonder fed the sick alpha the portion of the reindeer, when he ate it, the alpha was healed! From that day this particular reindeer is called healdeer.

Wonder didn't stay in his pack; he collected all the lone wolves and made his own pack. They all travelled to this mountain, and the pack lives peacefully with the name "adventurer"

"it's a nice story" Alaska remarked

"It happened in reality" wander told

"Yeah, its technically the history of our pack" frost agreed.

Pearl was silent, hearing about lone wolves made her remember what will happen to her. The full moon night was almost there and she hadn't hunted her reindeer.

There was absolutely <u>no way</u> she could hunt a healdeer.

"Can I stay here? With you all, I will be a lone wolf soon you know" Pearl asked, her voice radiating the sadness of her heart.

"WHAT?! You are going to be a lone wolf??" frost asked, his face whipped around to look at her.

"Yeah, I haven't found my inner power yet, so I can't hunt"

Alaska remembered with a start that Pearl was going to be a lone wolf, which meant she couldn't stay with him.

"I think you should try your howl" frost suggested

"How you know?" Pearl asked

"Your howl was different, just try one more time" frost explained.

Pearl smiled; she was blessed to have such nice friends.

"So, let's go to hunt!"

~~~~~~~~~~~~~~~~~~~
~~~~~~~~~~~~~~~~~~~

CHAPTER SEVENTEEN

Inner Powers

"The weather of the flower valley doesn't suit me" Alaska complained

"Me too" Pearl agreed.

"We just have to hunt and get out of here" wander said

They hide behind a bush and gaze at the herd, looking for a perfect deer.

"Remember, old or wounded, I think we must not hunt foals because they need a chance to live" frost told them.

"that's exactly what I think" Alaska agrees.

They soon found an old healdeer, busy grazing. When they tried to stalk it, the healdeer sensed them immediately and made a dash for its life. The wolves shot after it.

Pearl stopped when she saw that the healdeer ran too fast, instead she howled, for Storm; dying a horrible death, for Alaska; who failed his mission, for herself; forgotten and probably a lone wolf.

No! she never gave up, now what happened? Why?

Pearl felt a shot of power in her body, she ran like she never ran in her life, she jumped on the healdeer and

She did it. **PEARL. DID. IT!**

"I DID IT!" Pearl shouts

"YOU DID IT!" Alaska shouts back, equally happy.

"I really found my inner power" Pearl said, disbelieving in herself

"Yes, you did" frost joins in

"I'm not a lone wolf!" Pearl exclaims.

"YOUR HOWL IS YOUR INNER POWER!" Alaska shouts

They were ready to go back home. After wrapping up the meat in leaves, Pearl and Alaska got ready for the night, they were to leave tomorrow

"It was great meeting you all" Alaska thanks the pack adventurers

"We liked meeting you too"

The wolves lay inside the big cave, waiting for sleep to come, Alaska begin

"When I was hunting for my first reindeer, I found the lone wolf rule quite unfair"

Frost nods and spoke

"Yes, me too...I used to think a wolf is good in a way it is, it'll hunt when it will find the inner power, why put the wolf under pressure and kick it out of the pack when it can't hunt?"

Pearl asks "Alaska, this is the wolf law, right?"

"Yes" Alaska answers

"Who makes the wolf law?" Pearl questions again.

"Umm, well once in a year the alphas of all the wolf packs meet, they discuss about the rules and things, they make rules everyone finds fair, and remove the rules everyone finds unfair" Alaska explains

"You'll be an alpha in the upcoming meeting, it's quite near" wander reminds

"Yeah"

"Use your power wisely, you could talk about the lone wolf law" frost suggests

"that's what I was thinking, I'm sure many wolf packs must be finding that law unfair"

Pearl soon tunes out of the wolves' talk, and falls into a deep sleep after a tiring but an exciting day.

~~~~~~~~~~~~~~~~~~~
~~~~~~~~~~~~~~~~~~~

CHAPTER EIGHTEEN

Tunnel

"I can't wait to go home!" Pearl exclaims

Alaska takes the leaves which were wrapped on meat in his mouth, so he couldn't speak but nodded. frost led them back to the flower valley; he motioned them all to follow him to a cave there.

wander explains: "it's a sort of tunnel, it will lead us out of this mountain"

the wolves enter it.

Pearl looked around in the dark. She could see a small distant dot of light, but other then that it was dark. A pair of arctic foxes block their way

"Umm, well-what-umm" the male fox begins but stops.

"don't worry, we are just crossing this tunnel and will not harm any of your kind" Pearl reassures.

The arctic foxes nodded gratefully and scamper away to their borrows.

The wolves stop at a fork, there were two similar paths.

"Which one do we have to go?" Pearl asks

Everybody looks at frost, who replies; "Well-err I think, this one"

He sounded like the male fox they met earlier.

"Frost, are you sure it's this one? You know it's very urgent and we have to go back home, we will have no time to turn back if we choose the wrong way." Alaska said

"And if we turn back, it'll be too late" Pearl finishes.

"Don't worry, I'm sure it's this one" frost sounded unsure.

They all follow him to the path.

"What do you all usually eat?" Pearl asks frost

"We only eat when we are very hungry, usually rabbits" frost stops and lowers his voice before continuing "and arctic foxes-rarely- sometimes, if we're lucky we find a reindeer or two to hunt, but I'm not hungry right now"

"How do lone wolves know that they have to come here?" Alaska asks

"They don't know, sometimes if our pack is wandering somewhere else other than the mountains, we find some lone wolves and take them in" wander answers.

"That's very kind of you, providing companionship and safety to the wolves that are rejected" Pearl admires.

"Actully, the lone wolves are quite talented-for us atleast-once they discover their inner powers, they become the best hunters in the universe"

"Which pack are you from, frost?" Alaska asks

"I was born in this pack" Frost replies

"What about you wander?" Pearl questions

"I came from the claw pack-a small one it is- most of the wolves were rude to me for two reasons. Firstly, because I couldn't hunt, and secondly because I was grey and the wolves of my pack were white" wander replied

"But wolves are not supposed to be judging each other because of their colours!" Pearl exclaims

"My pack was different, in a bad way" wander explains, then continues "on the day I was announced as a lone wolf, most wolves seemed happy except my friend who also became a lone wolf soon, frost came and then we both joined the pack"

"Who was your friend?" Alaska asked

"Her name is pure, we're both mates now" wander answers, smiling to himself

"Glad to hear that!" Pearl exclaims

"I was actully happy that I became a lone wolf when I was accepted by the adventurers pack, the wolves in it were so friendly and easy-going, pure and me soon learnt to hunt, then I became frost's assistant and so I was treated with more respect, I'm really thankful to frost" wander explains.

"we're near the end of the tunnel" frost announced

~~~~~~~~~~~~~~~~~~~~
~~~~~~~~~~~~~~~~~~~~

CHAPTER NINETEEN

Home

They step out of the tunnel/cave, blinking in the sudden exposure to light.

"So now where we go?" Pearl asks, eyeing the sea-shore.

"Follow the sea-shore with the mountains on your back, you will soon reach the wolf grounds so halt!" wander tells, as if reciting.

"Nice" Pearl giggles.

Alaska-who had meat in his mouth-shook his head, but in a nice way.

The wolves march steady on, towards their destination.

"Who were your parents?" wander asks Pearl.

"My mom's name was Ava, and my father's name was howl, they are not alive now"

"Sad to hear that, what about you Alaska?" wander asked.

Alaska gives the meat to Pearl to hold so he could answer.

"Our family is the descendants of alphas, in other words it means that our generation used to be alphas, are alphas and will be alpha of the sunlight pack, my mom's name was snowball and my dad's name is Storm."

"I'm the descendant of wonder, the wolf in the story I told" frost explains

"What about you wander?" Pearl asks in a muffled voice because she was holding the meat.

"My mom's name was Alia, my father's name was Snow, they both died before I became a lone wolf." Wander answers.

"Oh!"

The sea crashed on the shore, anyone in the reach of those terrible waves would be swept in the sea, the wolves kept away from the sea.

Snow snow and snow, on their left was the sea. And other then that was the vast tundra of snow.

Some rabbits were scampering there and here.

Wander heard a howl, his ears pricked up.

Alaska heard a howl too, he stopped walking.

Frost heard a howl, he looked around.

Pearl heard a howl, she howled back.

Alaska howled with her, but frost and wander didn't join, instead they ran.

Alaska and Pearl followed, snow flying at their heels.

Then as they had started, they stopped abruptly.

"Now we have to go" frost said

"Why?" Pearl asked

"Because you are now in your home"

~~~~~~~~~~~~~~~~
~~~~~~~~~~~~~~~~

CHAPTER TWENTY

Heal

"What?" Pearl said, shocked

"Yes, the wolves' territories have started and we can't go any further" wander explained

"It seems like our territory" Alaska suggests.

"So, you both go your way and we both go our way" wander said

Alaska and Pearl gazed turned to frost and wander, without knowing it they all had became great friends, it was all silent until:

"So...I geuss see you again?" Pearl stammered

"Yes, see you soon" frost answered

"It was nice being your freinds" Alaska said

"And companions" Pearl added

"I hope your father heals soon" Frost offered

"And we hope safe journey to you all" Alaska wishes

Frost and his assistant turned their nozzles towards the north, the wolves stand side by side gazing at their new friends getting covered by the gathering mist, Pearl suddenly remembers and shouts

"COME HERE WHEN YOU ARE WANDERING ADVENTURERS!" and with that, Alaska and Pearl howled and waited for a reply, a howl came and an answer too "WE WILL!" or was it just the wind or an echo of their own voices?

"Oh god you are safe you are alive we were so worried" a pack member named coco said, he was an old rival of Pearl's but now he wasn't or so she thought.

"Hey hey slow down dude, how's the alpha?"

"Umm, yeah follow me" coco said, not answering Alaska's question.

How good its to be back, I hope Storm is alright Pearl thought

Coco leads them to the alpha's cave and laiba was the first to see them, she runs around announcing their arrival.

Storm lay in his cave, gasping, his eyes closed. Dark sat near him; his head bowed.

"There's nothing I can do" he said to coco, Alaska and Pearl weren't in the view.

"Alaska? Pearl!" dark spoke, startled when he saw them

"They came today" coco told dark.

"I'm so sorry about your father, he-he..." dark trails away

"But we brought the healdeer!" Alaska exclaims, pushing the package of the meat with his paw in front of dark.

"You passed the challenges? Am I dreaming? How is this possible?!" dark exclaims, springing to his feet and *looking* at Pearl and Alaska

"Yes, we did" Pearl says proudly, not the vain kind of proud, but the type of proud that comes after you got something you didn't think you would get, a kind of proud that comes before important moments.

Dark opened the leaves and sniffed at the meat, he nodded and beckoned Alaska to give the meat to his father, the other wolves- Laiba, coco, Pearl and others - watched with hushed breaths praying that the alpha gets alright.

Back to normal.

Alaska laid the meat near his father's nozzle, he whispered to Storm before backing away with Pearl.

"Dad, please, just eat...it's for you"

Storm opened his eyes and looked around, his gaze rested on Pearl and Alaska. Storm croaked

"You came then"

"I will explain you later, just eat" Alaska urges

Storm wolfed it down and slept.

"He will be better after he wakes up, you should both rest now" dark suggests.

Alaska slumps down besides his father-it was his den too-while Pearl goes to her pack with the excited she-wolves behind her.

"how did you escape the polar bears?"

"And how did you survive the harsh snowstorms?"

"And how did you climb the mountains?"

"How did you hunt the healdeer?"

Pearl turned around to look at the wolves and smiled kindly before saying

"I will answer questions with the rest of the pack, once Storm's free"

The wolves' nodded and Pearl turned to her den.

She rested for a while until she heard a voice from her den's entry, it belonged to Laiba

"Yes Laiba? Come in" Pearl permitted and sat on her hunches, Laiba came and sat across her, she whispered

"I'm sorry"

"I'm sorry about the time I bullied you, I thought you were worthless, I'm so sorry for being rude to you, but now I know I'm wrong to think you as worthless" Laiba apologized

Pearl replied "My past doesn't define me Laiba, I think you should stop judging wolves with their pasts, be kind to them before other than apologizing after"

"I know, I'm sorry"

"Not everybody will forgive you, but I think it will be good to make a freind" Pearl had forgiven Laiba.

"Thank you" she exclaimed

Pearl was about to reply but she was interrupted by a howl. Storm's howl.

"THE ALPHA!" Laiba gasped.

They both ran to the cave along with other wolves and saw Storm sitting in his haunches.

"I Feel better!"

~~~~~~~~~~~~~~~~~~~
~~~~~~~~~~~~~~~~~~~

Epilogue

2 Month Later

Her white paws skidded through the fresh snow. Her blue eyes were fixed on her prey that was a reindeer. The young reindeer ran for its life, its hoofs skidded baches of snow on her nozzle, but she didn't stop.

She was near her prey; very nearby.

Just one more leap, just one more leap.

She leaped and her work was done!

Coco came to her and whispered

"Lone wolf you hunted?" but not in a mean way

"Coco! My name is not lone wolf!" Pearl replied, annoyed

Pearl was not a lone wolf; she was the alpha along with Alaska. It was the rule that the main alpha (Alaska) needed a partner to run the pack, they were both mates now!

Pearl remembered the time Alaska and Pearl had told their story to the pack, how Storm had listened, how Laiba's ears had pricked up, expaisely when they had got to the part where Pearl had hunted the heal deer. How Alaska had given her a knowing wink when he cut the part in which they had met the adventurer's pack.

Pearl remembered the day she was announced as the co-alpha, every wolf of the pack was happy. When she had been called, coco who didn't know that Pearl had learned to hunt and thought she was being called because she was to be announced as a lone wolf had whispered;

"Bye lone wolf!"

And she had replied

"Say that again I didn't quite hear you, I have been at an adventure and have got my badge of honour, you messed with the wrong wolf in the wrong era, you don't know me properly!" and then she had marched to Alaska with coco looking very surprised.

"Hello?" coco said, bringing her out of her thoughts.

"Ok wolves! That's it for today I geuss! We have got more reindeers enough for the day!" Pearl ordered

Alaska nodded and spoke

"Great! You are getting hang of hunting and leadership"

"You are still better than me"

But Alaska was right, Pearl didn't need to howl to hunt.

They both look at each other and Alaska orders the wolves to take the reindeers back to the dens.

Alaska and Pearl walk togather silently

"It was an amazing adventure" Alaska remembered, he meant the journey to the flower valley

"And it was better because we were togather" Pearl remarked

"Do you miss the adventurers, Pearl?"

"Sometimes, because without their help we won't have been here" Pearl answered

"You are right"

The both climb up to the cliff and gaze at the setting sun, making the sky orangish. both wolves sat togather, silhouetted in the last of the rays of setting sun.

~~~~~~~~~~~~~~~

THE END
~~~~~~~~~~~~~~~

Author's Note

Hello! Its me, Sidra Khan!

This book was inspired by my love of wolves and the love for the arctic, though I have never visited that place, what I read about the place was enough!

I love wolves for their unity and strength and bravery, how they are very much like humans in behaviour.

This story took place in my mind randomly one day, the characters formed and I decided that this one wolf who was unique and lonely and in a danger of finishing, but then, a dangourous adventure unfolds and she has to go with her friend. This wolf, the star of the story would be Pearl and the friend would be Alaska.

This ritual of the sunshine pack, the deer hunting rule isn't really a real rule but I made it up, the lone wolf and everything is also a myth, but who knows? Maybe everything does exist and we don't even know!

Do you know- even though wolves are a close ancestor of the dog- wolves can't be tamed or pet? People do try to keep the majestic animals in their houses, but more or less they end up with some of their toes been eaten.

Most people don't realize this, but wolves are very much endangered like (literally) every animal out there. Deforestation and excessive hunting for their beautiful coats or just the sport of it is threatening wolves' lives very badly.

Most people think that wolves kill thousands of farmer's sheep and cattle every year and farmers starve because of them. But my dear friends, wolves do not kill the cattle, and if they do its very rare and is more or less related to the hunting of their food (deer, rabbits)

Wolves are a big part of the eco system, more of like a keystone species. When the wolves got extinct In the Yellowstone national park things go really very poorly.

I hope you enjoyed reading this book as much as I enjoyed writing it and you learned about wolves, because right now we need all the help we can in saving the animals.

A wolf Hug,

Sidra Khan

Acknowledgment

There are lots of people I want to say thanks to, so let's begin.

Thank you my amazing awesome encouraging parents who supported my every step and chapter, gave me suggestions. This book would'nt have been possible without you.

Thanks to my dad's side grandma for listening all I had to say about the book's charachters.

A big shoutout to Ayesha-yes you, my best friend- for giving me amazing ideas and reading my book for the first time ever and the amazing coversations we had about Pearl and Alaska.

Thanks to my other family members- My little brothers and everyone.

A big thanks to my english teacher who supported me and corrected my grammer.

A shoutout to all of the notion press team which helped me publish this book.

And most importantly, I am grateful for all of you who are readind this book, because without you, my readers this book would mean nothing.

Thank you everyone, you meant a lot for me and my book